To Lily
—A. A.

Henry Holt and Company, LLC
Publishers since 1866
175 Fifth Avenue
New York, New York 10010
mackids.com

Library of Congress Cataloging-in-Publication Data is available

ISBN 978-0-8050-9703-0

Henry Holt books may be purchased for business or promotional use.
For information on bulk purchases, please contact Macmillan Corporate
and Premium Sales Department at (800) 221-7945 x5442
or by email at specialmarkets@macmillan.com.

First Edition—2014 / Designed by April Ward
The illustrations for this book were done in pen and ink on vellum paper, then colored digitally.

Printed in China by Toppan Leefung Printing Co. Ltd.,
Dongguan City, Guangdong Province.
1 3 5 7 9 10 8 6 4 2

EDDA

A Little Valkyrie's First Day of School

Adam
Auerbach

Christy Ottaviano Books

Henry Holt and Company · New York

Edda is the littlest Valkyrie.

She lives in Asgard, a land
full of magic and adventure.

Edda's papa and her big sisters watch
over all of Asgard. Sometimes Edda helps
them search the land for unruly monsters.

But Edda doesn't want to only find monsters.

During her writing lessons, Edda's thoughts are
far away. "Papa," she says, "I want to find someone
my own age." Thankfully, her papa is very wise.
He knows of a place where she can meet other kids.

The next day, Edda and her papa fly all the
way to Earth for the first day of school.

Edda has never been away from Asgard.

"Don't worry," her papa says. "Valkyries are very brave."

"Even little Valkyries?" asks Edda.

"Yes, even little Valkyries," says Papa.

The classroom is full of new faces. Edda waits for someone to say hello, but no one does. She wishes she were back home in Asgard.

In Asgard, Edda can
do what she wants,

and go where she pleases.

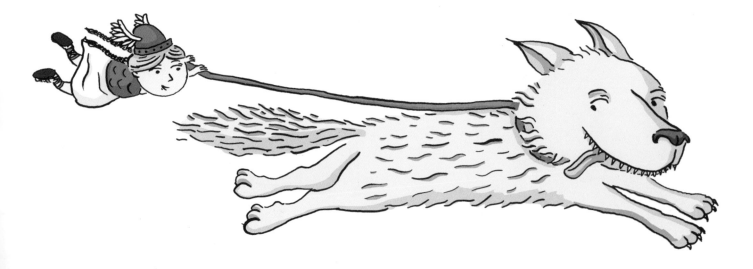

In school, she is
expected to sit still.

When she doesn't,
she gets time out.

In Asgard, each meal is a feast,
and everyone shares.

In school, no one wants to make a trade.

In Asgard, no one stands in Edda's way.

In school, she has to wait in line.

In Asgard, there are many amazing creatures.

At school, there is only Rex.

And at school there are writing assignments.

Edda decides to draw
a picture instead.

But her teacher says
she has to write something
in her journal.

Writing is hard work.

Edda starts to daydream about being back home in Asgard.

Then, she has an idea. She writes and writes, until the teacher calls on her.

"My story is about a magical place
called Asgard," Edda begins.

She tells a tale of **danger**,

bravery,

victory,

and **forgiveness**.

Edda's story is a big hit.

Everyone wants to learn
more about her life in Asgard.

When Edda's papa picks
her up after school, he picks
up one of her friends, too.

Together, they fly back to Asgard.

Edda and her new friend tell the creatures
of Asgard all about the first day of school.

Some of the creatures think it sounds wonderful.

The next day, Edda brings
a surprise along. "School looks
so different from Asgard,"
whispers the dragon.

"Don't worry," says Edda.
"Dragons are very brave."